Cupid's Revenge

By Sylvia McDaniel

Books by Sylvia McDaniel

Contemporary Romance

Standalones
The Reluctant Santa
My Sister's Boyfriend
The Wanted Bride
The Relationship Coach
Her Christmas Lie
Secrets, Lies, and Online Dating
Paying for the Past
Cupid's Revenge

Anthologies
Kisses, Laughter & Love
Christmas with you

Collaborative Series

Magic, New Mexico
Touch of Decadence

Western Historicals

Standalones
A Hero's Heart
A Scarlet Bride
Second Chance Cowboy

The Cuvier Women
Wronged
Betrayed
Beguiled

Lipstick and Lead
Desperate
Deadly
Dangerous
Daring
Determined
Deceived

Scandalous Suffragettes
Abigail
Bella
Callie
Faith

The Burnett Brides
The Rancher Takes a Bride
The Outlaw Takes a Bride
The Marshal Takes a Bride
The Christmas Bride

Anthologies
Wild Western Women
Courting the West
Wild Western Women Ride Again

Collaborative Series

The Surprise Brides
Ethan

American Mail Order Brides
Katie

Cupid's Revenge
Published by Virtual Bookseller

Cover Design by Kim Killion
thekilliongroupinc.com/

Formatting by Laurelle Procter
laurelleprocter@gmail.com

Short Description: Has he forgiven her for running from an elopement that would have resulted in a disastrous marriage? And has she gotten over the handsome cowboy?

ISBN: 978-1-942608-16-5 (paperback)
ISBN: 978-1-942608-13-4 (e-book)

{Contemporary Romance – Fiction}
{Western Romance – Fiction}

www.SylviaMcDaniel.com

Synopsis

Ten years ago, Skye Brand ran from Cupid, Texas to avoid marriage to Zane Calhoun. Now she's returning for the Valentine wedding of her friends Michelle and Ryan where she'll see Zane for the first time. Has he forgiven her for running from an elopement that would have resulted in a disastrous marriage? And has she gotten over the handsome cowboy?

Table of Contents

<h1 style="text-align:center">Chapter One</h1>

Entering the city limits of Cupid, Texas for the first time in ten years was like going to the dentist for a root canal. Painful and numbing. But Skye Brand wouldn't miss the Valentine Day wedding of her close friend, Michelle, though the event would be a happy occasion sprinkled with intermittent, agonizing remembrances of Zane Calhoun.

Michelle had informed her Zane was a groomsman in the wedding. Single and still hated Skye.

She glanced over in the car at her long-haired dachshund, Putz, who sat in his carrier, watching her drive. "It's just you and me, buddy. We don't need a man in our life."

Putz tilted his head and gazed at her with his beady brown eyes, trying to understand, gazing at her with unconditional love. Dogs were so easy compared to men. Food, water and love, and they were yours for life.

Skye stopped at the town's only stop light. A sign said High School State Football Champions and listed the years the local team reigned supreme in the state of Texas. Zane had played defensive end their senior year when they won State. The memory of that night felt like it happened yesterday. Yeap, this weekend would be like every dental nightmare all wrapped up in white wedding cake.

The town hadn't changed much in ten years. A new box store added at the edge of town, a fresh coat of paint on the local DQ and the cupid statue still sat in the town's square. What idiot thought a man in a diaper with a bow and arrow was cute?

She pulled up in front of The Cupid Love Nest, a bed and breakfast run by Mabel Underwood, who could spread secrets faster than the internet. A white Victorian two story home surrounded by a wrap-around porch adorned with rocking chairs was the town's only bed and breakfast. The house belonged in a different era and gazing at the older home Skye wondered what she was doing back in Cupid.

After waffling for months about whether or not to return for Michelle's wedding, Mabel's was the only place she'd been able to get a room. Michelle's large family had sold out the only decent hotel in town and Skye refused to stay at the Valentine Express where rooms were rented by the hour.

Skye parked the car, took Putz out of his carrier and put his leash on him. She grabbed her suitcase, the make-up bag that held the tools of her trade, and started up the steps.

A gray-haired Mabel met her at the door, her reading glasses tilted on the end of her nose. "I'm sorry, we're all booked up this weekend.

"I have a reservation."

Mabel frowned at the dog. "No pets."

"Mabel, its Skye Brand. I made a reservation a month ago and you sent me an email saying I could bring my dog."

"That girl from Cupid High School, whose parents were killed in that horrible crash out on highway 67?"

Skye tensed. Was the tragic death of her parents the only thing people remembered about her?

"Skye Brand, make-up artist and stylist. Former Valedictorian for the class of 2002," Skye said regretting she'd only received a thousand dollar scholarship for college.

"Well come on in, honey, I didn't recognize you with your hair all colored and frizzed like that," Mabel said, as she opened the door.

Skye's short hair had blonde tips and she'd put enough mouse in it to make her appear like she'd juiced up on electricity first thing this morning. According to Vogue the spiked look was the latest fashion. She'd wanted her return to reflect she was no longer that small town girl who'd left numb with grief and fear. She'd brought the latest big city hairdo home to Cupid.

She stepped over the threshold and entered the big house with Putz right behind her.

Mabel stared at her dachshund, her frame bent over. "He's had all his shots and he doesn't have fleas, does he?"

"All shots and no fleas."

"Okay," she said hesitation in her voice. "I need you to sign this paperwork. Breakfast is from seven thirty to nine. That's the only meal I provide. What brings you back to town?"

"Michelle Cooper's wedding. I'm doing her hair and make-up."

Mabel frowned at her. "I hope you don't intend to style her hair like yours. Maybe that's what those women in Dallas wear, but it needs a good combing."

"This is Michelle's day and I'll fix her hair however she wants," Skye said, wanting to tell Mabel her hair style was the latest fashion.

"Michelle's got good sense. She's marrying that Vanderbilt boy."

Skye didn't say anything. She'd been shocked when Michelle announced her engagement to Ryan. They just didn't seem to go together. But if that was who her friend chose to marry, she'd support her decision.

"I'm putting you in the Cupid Bow room, since you're not wearing a wedding ring and no man is with you. Maybe the ambiance of the room will help you find true love," Mabel said handing her the key.

Mabel hadn't changed. Still outspoken with little or no tact, a mouth the size of a megaphone with enough connections in town to blast gossip in minutes. Within the hour, Skye's return to Cupid would be all over town.

"Mabel, you're too kind," Skye said. But the sarcasm was lost on the innkeeper.

"Keep your dog on a leash. My Scottie recently had surgery, so I'm trying to keep her quiet. She's getting old and grumpy."

Not unlike her owner, Skye thought. Maybe there was something to people looking and acting like their pets. She glanced down at Putz. Yep, the patch of long blonde hair on the top of his head stood straight up, matching her own.

"Your room's at the top of the stairs, two doors down and on the right."

"Thanks," Sky said, juggling her bags.

Skye carried her suitcase and makeup bag upstairs with Putz following obediently. Later, she would get his carrier and bring that up as well, but right now she just wanted to unpack, call Michelle, settle in and relax.

An hour later, she descended the stairs eager to take Putz for a well-deserved walk. She'd changed into her jogging outfit, her short spiky blonde hair still stood on end and she'd brushed a new coat of striking hot pink lipstick across her lips. Later tonight, the plans were to meet her girlfriends from school and catch up. Putz trailed down the stairs behind her. When they reached the entry way, she turned to her faithful dachshund.

"Do you wanna go for a walk?"

He danced around in circles, barking. She snapped the leash on his collar and he raced towards the door almost dragging her.

It was then she glanced up into the searing brown-eyed gaze she'd dreaded seeing. She froze, staring at how much he'd changed. How the boy had become a man and she almost quit breathing.

"Zane," she said, in a breathless rush, her body betraying her by reacting to the sight of the boy she'd once loved. Six feet of long, tall Texan with a six-pack of abs and those whiskey brown eyes, that could ignite a flame low in her belly stood before her.

"Skye," he acknowledged.

"What are you doing here?" she asked, her heart jumping at the thought that he'd come for her. Remembering the years she'd waited hoping he would come find her. Waited hoping he'd realize she sacrificed their love so that he could attend college.

"Ms. Underwood's terrier had surgery a couple of days ago. I'm checking on her."

She paused feeling foolish. What the hell was she thinking? He'd never searched for her. Never--and it still hurt. She'd waited for him, hoping and dreaming that once he finished college, he'd return and they would start over. But that was the past. She needed to move on.

"So you're a vet?"

"Yes," he said his tone short and terse.

"Congratulations, you achieved your dream," she said, determined to smile and never let him know how much he'd hurt her, even if it killed her. And it almost did.

"Yes."

He squatted down to pet Putz. "You're a little excited, aren't you boy?"

"We're going for a walk. He loves his daily walk."

Putz moaned and strained on the leash, trying to move Skye toward the door.

Zane rubbed the dog behind the ears. Never one to pass up a belly rub, Putz dropped down to the floor and rolled over. "Ah, I found your favorite spot."

"He loves to have his belly rubbed."

The dog licked him on the hand and Skye thought *traitor*. This was the enemy. This was the man who blamed her for their break-up.

She pulled on the leash. "Come on, Putz. We need to go before it gets dark."

The dog rose to his feet and so did Zane. His gaze met hers for the first time since their initial glance.

"I guess you're here for the wedding."

"Yes," she replied.

"I'll try to stay out of your way, if you do the same for me. That way we won't ruin Michelle and Ryan's wedding."

Stunned, she stared at him amazed at the audacity of the man. He thought she would create a scene and ruin her friend's wedding? He thought a little too highly of himself, if he thought she still cared.

"Not a problem. I would never create a scene that would hurt my friend. What happened between us was years ago. I'm over it."

"Even if I told the whole town what a little liar you are?"

She bristled, but remained determined to take the high road. "Good to see you again, Zane."

Skye, walked out the door, with Putz pulling at the leash. Tears cascaded down her face and she wanted to run. How could it still hurt after all these years? She wasn't a liar and if he knew the truth, he would be thanking her.

Chapter Two

The next morning, Skye stood in the bathroom, finishing her makeup. She wasn't used to a day off. She pretty much worked whenever she had a client who needed their hair or make-up done. Over the years, her client list had grown until her business was large enough to support her.

Today she planned to drive by the old home place, visit her parent's graves, and do a little shopping. Then later tonight she'd meet friends after the rehearsal dinner. It'd been great to visit with her girlfriends last night, except listening to all the comments about Zane. She'd refused to take the bait and not mentioned him once. It still hurt that Zane thought she'd lied to him.

It hadn't exactly been a lie. She'd left town after promising him that they could run off and get married. When he'd learned she was broke and homeless after her parent's unexpected death, he'd wanted them to marry. Finally, after he refused to take no for an answer she'd agreed to the marriage. But she wouldn't let him give up his dream for her.

Overwhelmed, she'd run from Zane and marriage. When he arrived at Michelle's to pick her up, Skye was halfway to Dallas.

After she arrived in Dallas, she'd called him, but he'd refused to speak with her. Now ten years later, Zane still hated her.

Skye left the bathroom and walked down the hall to her room where the door stood ajar. She pushed the door open, noticing that Putz's carrier was empty. Crap, this couldn't be good. She threw on some clothes and just as she started down the stairs, she heard screaming from the back of the house.

"Get off, Sassy. Get away from her, you mangy dachshund."

The squeal of Putz yelping in pain had her running toward the sound.

"What's wrong?" Skye cried, as she came around the corner into the personal quarters where Mabel lived.

She sat holding her dog on her lap.

"Your dog attacked my little Sassy. He bit her on the nose, but she got him back."

Putz was hiding under the table. "Come here, baby. It's all right," Skye called. She held out her hand and coaxed him to her.

"I'm sorry. I don't know why, but he bites the nose of every dog he meets. He's not vicious, I think it's his way of saying hello."

"He can't stay here. I can't have Sassy being bothered while she's recovering."

"Oh my God, he's bleeding. She bit him on the back of the neck," Skye cried, gazing at the open wound on Putz's neck. He lay at her feet, his body shivering. "Poor baby."

Mabel came over and glanced at Putz's neck. "She got him good. You need to take him over to Dr. Calhoun's office."

Skye frowned. Just who she didn't want to see. Zane. If she didn't know any better, she would believe that Mabel had done this on purpose just to get the two of them together.

"Do you have a clean cloth I can put on his neck to keep him from bleeding everywhere?"

Mabel brought her one. "I think maybe you should board him at Zane's. That way we won't have this problem again."

"I'm only here two more nights. I promise he'll stay in my room, in his crate."

Mabel shook her head. "Nope, I don't want to take a chance with Sassy's health. If you can't find another room, then you're going to have to board him."

"You know there are no other hotel rooms in town."

"Then I guess you'll just have to board him at Dr. Calhoun's vet hospital."

Skye picked up Putz and carried him to the car, where she gently laid him in the front seat. After she retrieved her purse and keys, she drove to the location.

She pulled in front of an old house that had been converted into a veterinary clinic. A sign in the yard, proclaimed the Calhoun Veterinary Hospital.

Putz trembled in her arms as she carried him inside. As she opened the door she could see the house had been gutted and a shiny modern clinic with a small reception area was housed inside the older frame. A young girl sat behind the receptionist desk.

"I'm sorry but we're about to close."

"My dog has been injured, I need Zane to take a look at him."

The girl's brows rose at her casual use of Zane's name. "I'm sorry, miss, but he's leaving."

"Please tell him Skye Brand is here and she needs his help." Skye wasn't certain that wouldn't get her kicked out faster, but she had to try to reach Zane before he left.

The girl rolled her eyes, picked up the phone and spoke into it. "I'm sorry, Dr. Calhoun, but Skye Brand is here. She has a vet emergency."

"I told her. But…oh my God, her dog is dripping blood on the floor. Yes, sir, I will."

"Follow me," the receptionist said as she led Skye down the hall.

The receptionist led Skye into an examining room. She put the trembling dachshund up on a table, while the girl walked out.

Zane entered from the other side of the room. "Nothing has changed. It's always an emergency with you, Skye."

"Sassy, Mabel's dog, took exception to Putz biting her on the nose."

"That old terrier?"

"Yes," Skye said, petting Putz to reassure her pet that everything would be okay, though his whole body trembled.

Zane gazed at the wound on Putz's neck. He spread it apart gently, while Skye held Putz.

Standing this close to Zane, her mind was tripping on his pheromones. That familiar aroma of man had her swaying as memories of the two of them kissing until their lips were swollen flooded her mind. They'd been so young. So in love.

"If you're going to faint, you can leave the room right now. I'm not catching you," he said, not taking his eyes off Putz.

Sky wanted to pinch herself. There had been other men in her life since Zane, but her body had always responded to him. It infuriated her that nothing had changed. Every cell in her body seemed to cry out for his.

"I don't faint."

"Oh Buddy, she took a bite out you." Zane said gazing into the open wound. He glanced at Skye. "Do you think you can hold him, while I clean this wound?"

"Yes."

"You won't let him go when he starts fighting me? Or get queasy and throw up."

"I can hold him," she said, gazing at Putz who was panting even though it was cold outside. "Is he going to be okay?"

"Yes. We just need to clean him up a bit and cover that bite." Zane held onto Putz's neck. "Okay, hang on, here we go."

Zane took out a bottle of what looked like an antiseptic wash and poured it into the wound.

Putz groaned, pulled and tugged trying to get away, but Skye held on tight. When he settled down, Zane took some liquid bandage poured onto the wound and put two strips across it to hold it together. Then he wrapped blue sticky gauze across Putz's neck and shoulder, covering the wound.

"Okay, you're all set."

"Uh, there's one other small detail," Skye said, staring into Zane's brown eyes, wishing he still looked at her with longing like he had so many years ago. "Mabel won't let me bring him back. He's been evicted from the bed and breakfast."

Zane rubbed Putz's ears. "You can't bite other dogs on the nose. It's not nice."

Skye resisted the urge to tell Zane that refusing to speak to her when she'd called all those years ago wasn't nice either, but she thought it best not to cause problems when she needed him to board her dog.

"We can board him here for the weekend. Besides I was going to give you some antibiotics to make sure that wound doesn't get infected. This way I can administer them while I watch over him."

"How much?"

"Twelve dollars a night."

She cuddled Putz to her. "I'm sorry, buddy. But you have to stay here."

Putz licked her on the chin and she held him against her for a moment, feeling guilty. First, the dog accident and now this. She was a horrible doggie mama.

"You'll take good care of him."

Zane stared at her, like she'd asked the stupidest question on the planet. He lifted Putz off the table sitting him on the floor. "It's not the dog's fault that you left me behind for a modeling job in Dallas."

"It wasn't a modeling job."

"Oh, a stripper?"

"That's just mean. I'm a stylist."

He walked around the examining table, placed both arms on either side of her, effectively blocking her in. A thrill of excitement sent a shiver down her spine. He leaned in close and for a moment she thought he was going to kiss her. She could feel his breath on her face and tilted her head to receive his mouth, wondering what it would feel like after all this time.

Zane pulled back as if he'd suddenly remembered she was public enemy number one. "Let's get one thing straight. I'm helping your dog, not you."

"Thank you, Zane," she said, resisting the urge to reach out and trace his lips with her finger.

The tight lines of tension etched in his face eased. He appeared confused by her kindness and took a step back putting distance between them.

Zane glanced down at his watch. "I've got to go. I have a final fitting for my tux in an hour."

He grabbed Putz's leash. "I'll let you back into the clinic on Sunday, so you can take him with you when you leave Cupid. You are leaving, right?"

"Sunday. I don't want to be here anymore than you want me here."

"I never said that."

"But you thought it," Skye said as she leaned down to rub Putz on the head.

"Don't forget to pay the receptionist on the way out."

She turned and walked out the door. The asshole wouldn't even be a vet if it weren't for her.

Chapter Three

Zane watched as Skye left his clinic. She drove off in a new Mustang convertible, its hefty engine roaring out of his parking lot. God, she was even more beautiful than she'd been at eighteen. Large and soft, her emerald eyes still had the power to increase his heart-rate. And her curves had matured into a shapely woman that he ached to explore.

He'd given her his heart, promised to take care of her and love her forever, but when she left town without even saying goodbye, her leaving ripped his tender organ into shreds. At first, he'd refused to go to college, but his mother hadn't given him any other options. Go to college or move out and get a job.

So he'd driven out of town, leaving Cupid in the rearview mirror to Texas A&M where he'd put his broken heart and soul into becoming a vet.

Now ten years later, he'd returned to Cupid. Skye had returned home at least until Sunday and with her homecoming, the pain of their parting flashed back resurrecting that emptiness in the middle of his chest. Maybe this time, it was his turn to show her how arriving to pick up your bride only to find her gone, ripped your insides into ground heartache. Maybe this time, he should tempt her into his bed and then send *her* down the road with Cupid in the rearview mirror. With a hole in her heart the size of Texas.

Maybe he should quit acting like an ass and show her he'd become a gentleman.

Chapter Four

Skye stood just inside Valentino's bar, the only honky tonk in town. She'd reserved twenty seats for the impromptu reunion of friend's and the wedding party. Michelle had invited her to the rehearsal dinner, but she'd refused. She wanted to style her friends hair, do her make-up and watch the wedding from the sidelines. The bigger her role in the wedding party, the more she would have had to interact with Zane. She didn't want or need any reminders of what they'd lost.

The party arrived with the bride looking exhausted, while the groom smiled. Zane came in behind Ryan and she admired the way he stood tall and handsome, his muscular body nicely filled out his dress jeans and western shirt. She'd forgotten how western wear wrapped a man up in a rugged manly package. On his feet were a pair of Nocona handcrafted boots, a size thirteen. She'd never forgotten.

"Hi," he said, walking up to her. "Putz sent a lick for you. Do you want it now or later?"

She shook her head at him. "No, thanks."

"I checked on him before I left tonight. He was resting comfortably, though he seems a little sad."

Skye closed her eyes, missing her dog. "Poor baby. He'll be okay?"

"Good as new in a few days," he said moving closer to her.

"I should have made certain the door was closed before I went to take my shower. He's always been curious."

"He probably smelled Sassy and wanted to go check her out."

What in the hell had gotten into him? They were talking

like two old friends.

She stared up at him. "Have you been drinking?"

He shrugged. "We had a couple of toasts of champagne tonight, but I'm sober. Why?"

"We're talking like friends."

A smile spread across his handsome face and even reached his eyes, warming his gaze. "Look, what happened was in the past. We need to move on. How about a truce until after the wedding? Then we can return to hating one another."

"I don't hate you," she said softly, wishing she could tell him how much she still missed him.

"What are you drinking?" he asked, changing the subject.

"White wine. A Pinot Grigio."

"Very impressive. Living in the big city has turned you into a wine connoisseur."

"Hardly. I can sip the wine slowly without the alcohol affecting me."

He grinned. "You couldn't hold your liquor in high school either."

"I never wanted to," she said, remembering how she'd refused to drink much, fearing alcohol. Even now she had a healthy respect for liquor.

He nodded. "That's true. But you remember that night we all went out to the lake and you and I took a blanket and we went around the bend…"

Her cheeks flamed. They'd almost done the deed that night. They'd come very close. If their friends hadn't found them, she probably would never have left Cupid a virgin.

But later that summer, her parents had been killed and everything changed.

"You're blushing," he said, leaning closer to her, his voice low and husky, caressing her.

"No, it's just warm in here. I thought you were going to

order us a glass of wine?" Not really wanting the wine so much as wanting his attention focused on something besides her.

"Coming right up," he said. He sauntered over to the waitress and ordered their drinks.

God, he still had the power to make her mind stop working. At a mere touch, she wanted to shred her clothes and get naked. What was wrong with her? The man hated her. Thought she'd done him wrong.

There should be a country song written about how Zane had been wronged. Like hell, she'd done him a favor. Kept him from a marriage he would have regretted. A marriage doomed for divorce. A marriage she'd wanted, yet knew the timing was all wrong.

He returned with a glass of wine for her and a bottle of beer for him then sank down next to her. She felt his gaze check her out.

"What are you doing?" she asked, feeling off kilter. He wasn't acting the way he had this afternoon. He wasn't acting like she was a wanted criminal and he intended to drag her to jail by her hair.

"I'm just checking out how you've changed over the years. You look good," he said. When his voice held that low timber when they were younger, they'd have been making out soon.

"You don't appear too shabby yourself."

"Your hair, though. Gosh I use to run my fingers through those long curls and pull you to me. Remember?"

She wanted to kick him. Of course she remembered. He would hold her head while his lips explored her mouth, turning her muscles into jelly and her insides into a raging inferno.

"I'm a stylist. This cut is the latest fashion," she said, ignoring his comment about their past. She took a deep gulp of her wine, needing to cool off. Why couldn't she turn off these memories?

"Yeah, Michelle told me you were doing her and the bridesmaid's hair and make-up. I can't wait to see what you do."

"I work for one of the top salons in Dallas," she said proud of how she'd built up her clientele. Today, she earned a good living.

"Let me get you another class of wine," he said, leaving to find the waitress.

What was she doing? She needed a clear head to do her best work tomorrow. She needed to show the town that there was more to her than just a sad little orphan girl.

Zane returned to her side and pulled his chair up close to hers. She looked him over. He was up to something. He'd gone from freezing her with his disdain, to turning up the charm. And she'd experienced that charisma before. It could have her near naked in little or no time.

"Are you trying to get me drunk?" she asked.

A smile played at the edges of his mouth. "What if I am?"

"It's not going to work."

A slow lazy grin spread across his face. "We'll see."

They stared at one another in a defiant test of wills as their gazes clashed. Finally she broke off the staring contest. Unsure as to who won.

"How was college?" she asked, not knowing what else to say to him.

"Good. Lots of studying, but I came out all right. And now I have my clinic."

"Yes, you do," Skye said, knowing he never would have gotten this far if she'd married him.

He picked up her left hand. "I don't see a wedding band."

Skye picked up his left hand. "Right back to you. Why haven't you married?"

"I got burned really bad right before I left for college. I haven't trusted women since."

She stared into his brown eyes, trying to see if he'd forgiven her. "So you became gay?"

He almost spewed his beer. "Hardly. I learned to keep my distance."

Skye dropped his hand, feeling nervous. She laid her hand on the table and he immediately covered her small one with his. It was a silly childish game they'd played as kids. Who would be the last one on top? She pulled hers out and placed it on top of his. He pulled his hand out and placed it on top of hers.

For a moment she stared at the way his hand covered her smaller one.

"You know some people say that this is foreplay," he said.

Shivers danced the tango along her spine.

She pulled her gaze away from their hands and stared into the warmth of his whiskey brown eyes. Though things were tense between them, they were still good together.

"How is this foreplay?"

"We're wrestling with who is going to be on top."

She laughed. The idea totally ridiculous. "We're not going to have sex."

He leaned in closer, grabbed her chair and pulled her in so that her chair was right between his legs. "But we could."

A hot electrical pulse zipped through her body, causing her breathing to become short and shallow at the idea of the two of them naked in bed together. She picked up the glass of wine and drank from it, letting the cool liquid ease down her throat, trying to find some way to escape the heat the idea of the two of them together created.

She smiled at him. "You hate me."

He shook his head, leaned in close and nuzzled her

neck. She didn't stop him, though part of her was screaming, *make him stop, make him stop*, another part of her was saying *let him go lower*.

"I don't hate you. I just…let's not talk about the past. Let's focus on tonight."

"But then there's tomorrow. And you'll still hate me tomorrow."

He pulled back, his eyes stared into hers. His finger reached out and trailed down her cheek, in a lingering caress. "Can you just live for the moment? Have you ever thought about how great sex could have been for us? We were young, but you know when we were together, it was explosive between us."

That internal flame that he always lit glowed through her body, leaving her breathless. He placed his hand in the small of her back and pulled her toward him. She knew he was going to kiss her and she both wanted and dreaded his mouth on hers.

His mouth covered hers. Unable to stop herself, she leaned into him, her body falling back into the rhythm that existed between the two of them. He guided her into his embrace as he traced her lips with his tongue. Her mouth opened for his along with her body as she welcomed him into her arms.

A country ballad about lost love played in the background. Their friends laughed and talked, while their lips got reacquainted.

The kiss ignited the heat that had already been simmering. She pulled away, her lips regretting the absence of his, but they stood in a bar with surrounded by friends. She opened her eyes to meet his heated gaze.

"Let's go," he said his voice husky.

She picked up her wine glass, needing a moment to think. If she left with him, they would have sex. He never mentioned he cared about her. If she left with him, she knew she would be taking a huge risk of him destroying her heart. But if she didn't take the chance, wouldn't she regret missing this opportunity?

Wasn't this what she'd always dreamed of? Hadn't she wondered what it would be like to have made love to Zane? Was there a chance this night could heal them?

Oh shit. She was risking everything.

She downed the wine. "My car is at the B&B. You're driving."

"Let's go."

Zane threw money down on the table. They left the bar, their friends gaping at them. They knew what they were doing. They knew they were going to have sex.

Chapter Five

Zane took her back to his place, unable to face Mabel Underwood. He drove his Ford F150 well over the speed limit, hurrying before Skye changed her mind. Determined to have her and then let her go. This was for tonight only. Tonight would not heal the wounds of their past, but it might even the score.

And answer one of the many questions that had haunted him these last ten years. What would it be like to make love to Skye Brand?

He parked the truck and hurried to open Skye's door.

"You still live with your mother?"

He laughed. "Hardly. No, she's living in a retirement center where she dances on Friday nights, plays bingo and goes on senior citizen cruises. She hardly ever visits Cupid."

For a moment, he feared Skye would back out, and demand he return her to the Cupid's Love Nest. But she marched up the steps to his home, like they were still seventeen.

After opening the door, he turned on the light and led her inside. Not bothering to linger, he grabbed her hand pulling her up the stairs to the master suite.

Upstairs, he didn't waste time and took her into his arms. "Do you want anything to drink?"

"Oh no, I've had way more than I should have. I'm here with you."

For a moment, he stared at her, not moving. "Are you saying that you wouldn't be here if you hadn't drank?"

"No, I'm saying my better judgment might have won if I had been completely sober."

His mouth lowered onto hers and he kissed her, his lips

moving over hers greedily. He plundered her lips, devouring her with a fierceness he hadn't experienced in years. This is where she should have been ten years ago. Here in his bed, as his wife. She wrapped her arms around him, pulling him tightly to her, matching his ardor. Her breasts were crushed against his chest and he wanted her naked in the next five minutes. Too many years had passed and he needed to see her now.

His mouth moved over hers, falling naturally back into a rhythm that existed between the two of them. A rhythm he'd never found with anyone else.

She begin to unbutton his shirt, her mouth never leaving his as her hands found their way to his chest. Her touch was like magic, as her fingers caressed his skin, leaving behind a trail of fire.

The girl he remembered was never this bold. The woman in his arms went after what she wanted. And she wanted him. With a tug, she yanked his shirt completely out of his pants and undid the button on his jeans. She slipped her hands down inside the front of his pants. A hot branding sensation overcame him as her fingers grasped his penis.

A deep moan escaped his throat. Why did they have this reaction to one another? Why had he never experienced sensual pleasure like this with any other woman? Why only with Skye?

When her hands reached his buttocks, he broke the kiss and stepped back out of her reach.

"Your turn," he said, and removed her sweater in one swift movement over her head.

She unfastened her jeans, while Zane sank down on the bed and yanked his boots and socks off. Quickly he shed his jeans.

A moment later, he stood before her naked, his penis jutting out proudly before him at full attention.

In lace panties and bra, Skye turned to face him.

"You don't need this," he said releasing the clasp of her bra. The garment slide down her arms to reveal her sweet full breasts with pink nipples puckered in a rosy shadow. She slipped her panties down her long legs and then stepped out of them.

God, she was beautiful. Even better than his teenage dreams.

He took her hand and led her to the bed, where he pulled her down beside him needing to feel her naked skin next to his. "We don't have to worry about parents walking in."

"Or anyone finding out," she said softly.

For some strange reason, he glanced at the clock. "Happy Valentine's Day."

Skye rolled over and threw her leg over his, her foot caressing his skin, while she placed her hand on his penis. "Happy Valentine's Day to you. Show me if my dreams of us together are as good as the real thing."

"You dreamed of us together like this?"

She placed her lips around his nipple and nipped him with her teeth. "Oh yes."

His mouth found hers again. The thought of her dreaming of the two of them together made him want to give her the best night of her life. For so long he'd tried to block her from his mind and his heart. And tonight she was breaking down walls he'd erected years ago, leaving him vulnerable once again.

His fingers found her hardened nipple and he stroked the tip until she moaned with pleasure. Bending over he took her breast in his mouth, pulling at her nipple. With a moan he released her breast and let his hand skim down her naked stomach. When he reached between her legs to the slicken folds of her womanly center, she clung to him as he coaxed her intimately with his fingers.

He wanted to give her pleasure. He needed her to feel as he did, desire spiraling out of control.

He didn't understand why he felt like he belonged here with this woman. Like he'd come home. Like he'd been lost in the wilderness and now she'd rescued him.

"Zane, please," she cried.

He reached over to the nightstand and pulled out a foil packet. Quickly he ripped it open and rolled the protection over his penis.

When he turned back, she wrapped herself around him, centering his penis at the opening of her womanhood. And he didn't hesitate. He pushed inside her, reeling from the tightness that surrounded him. His blood pounded from the need to possess her, to push into her womanly sheath over and over until she cried out his name.

Why couldn't he rid himself of the need for this woman? Their hips moved in sync with fierceness, intensity and a rhythm that surprised him. With each stroke, she raised her hips to meet him, driving his pleasure closer to the edge. Passion filled him until he thought he would burst from the desire only Skye seemed to evoke.

With no other woman had he ever experienced such desire--such need. Like a cliff rushing toward him, he burst over the edge, carrying Skye with him as they came crashing down to earth together.

For a moment they lay, stunned, their breathing harsh and noisy as they recovered.

"That was nothing like I'd ever dreamed about," she finally said, her breathing fast. "It was better."

Zane lay spent, wondering what in the hell he'd just done. How did he tell her goodbye, when she'd clearly imprinted herself onto his heart? Yet she'd left him once, who was to say she wouldn't again

Chapter Six

Skye awoke the next day with sunshine streaming through the curtains, wrapped around Zane's hard male body. She glanced at the clock and sat straight up.

"Crap," Skye said, jumping out of bed and searching for her clothes. "I have to be at the church in an hour to do the bridesmaids hair."

Zane rolled over and watched her as she threw on her clothes.

"Get up. You have to drive me to the bed and breakfast," she said, pulling on her pants.

There was a moment of silence before he sat up in bed, his gaze fixated on her.

"You can walk to the B&B it's only three blocks over," he said, his voice chilly.

She glanced at him. The warm lover of last night was gone. He sat in bed, a sheet pulled to his waist, his eyes colder than a Texas norther.

"What's wrong?" she asked, a strange sense of impending doom coming over her. Last night she'd had hope, but this morning that seemed like a dream that the sunlight burned away.

He smiled. "Thanks for last night. Anytime you're in town, call me and we can get together for a quickie."

She stopped, shame spreading through her like a wildfire. He'd used her and this morning his true colors were no longer hidden. "What about last night? It was like old times. What about us?"

"There is no us. You ended that ten years ago when you left without saying goodbye. At least I'm saying goodbye." He smiled and crossed his arms across his chest. "Hurts doesn't it?"

She stared at him wanting to kick and punch him, but determined not to let him see how much his words knifed through her.

"You don't think the day I left Cupid and moved to Dallas wasn't the hardest thing I've ever done. You don't think that every time the door opened, I hoped it was you coming to get me?"

She stood and walked over to his side of the bed, fighting the tears that threatened to choke her. "You don't think that after you completed your veterinary training, I felt so proud of you and prayed you would show up at my door.

For eight years, I waited for you. And then last night after what we experienced, I thought you would realize that what we have is special. But you're too stupid."

"You didn't have to leave town."

"Oh no, I could have stayed and then you would never have gone to college and become the vet you dreamed of since you were a boy. We would have been two kids, broke, trying to raise a family, and get by with nothing. Instead, I left so that you could achieve your dream. So forgive me for putting your needs first. Forgive me for knowing that eventually you would have hated me for keeping you from going to school. Forgive me for dying inside while you went to college and I worked two jobs, to go to beauty school."

It was no use. She stopped for a moment and he lay there staring at her, a frown on his face.

"I'm done. I thought maybe we were given a second chance to get it right, but instead you just wanted revenge. I hope your revenge keeps you warm at night."

She turned and ran out of his bedroom hurrying down the stairs.

"Skye, wait!"

She heard him call after her.

"Go to hell!" she cried as she slammed the door behind her.

Tears cascaded down her cheeks as she ran the three blocks to the B&B. No hope of reconciliation. No hope of forgiveness. They were done.

Chapter Seven

Zane stood at the door and watched Skye running down the street. He closed the door and glanced around the room. The silence was deafening as he walked into the kitchen and saw their ice cream bowls sitting on the sink. Last night they'd shared the last of his cherry vanilla ice cream, laughing and giggling as they'd deliberately dropped spoonfuls on each other's naked bodies, licking the melting cream off of strategic body parts. They'd laughed and played just like they were kids again. The night was one of the best of his life, yet this morning he'd deliberately hurt her, wanting her to experience the pain he'd felt.

But was she right? Would he have hated her for getting in the way of him becoming the only thing he'd ever dreamed of being in life? What if he wasn't a vet? What would he have done in this small town that he'd never wanted to leave?

He'd planned on becoming a vet since the time he was ten years old. Since the day he'd brought home his dog, Rusty, with a broken leg and nursed him back to health. Since that time, Zane had known he loved animals and wanted to heal them.

Was she right to let him go off to college? Did she really think he would search for her?

But he hadn't looked for her. He'd gone to college and blamed her for his heartache. Why hadn't he skipped school to go after her, unless he knew she was right? Unless subconsciously he wanted to achieve his dream.

After her parent's death, she had nothing, no home, no college fund, no money, nothing but her clothes. He'd wanted to shelter and protect her. He'd promised her they'd get married and she'd argued against it until finally he'd worn her down. But when he arrived to pick her up at Michelle's where she was staying, Skye was gone.

Michelle told him that Skye's aunt had taken her home to Dallas. That Skye needed time to grieve and heal.

Had he been so stubborn he couldn't see that Skye was right? She'd been shell shocked at the sudden, unexpected death of her parents. He wanted to go to college and become a vet. She needed time to grieve.

Marrying Skye straight out of high school would have kept him from his dream. And though they loved one another at the time, would it have been enough to keep them together?

Young marriages had a high-rate of divorce. Especially when neither of you had a job that could support the two of you.

He'd never considered for a moment that she might have been hurting when she left without saying goodbye. And then when she called to explain, he wouldn't talk to her.

Had she sacrificed their relationship so that he could become the man he was today?

Damn! No matter what, there would always be a place on his heart with Skye's imprint. Last night had proven the chemistry between them was just as explosive today as ten years ago. And today of all days--Valentine's Day--the day of hearts and flowers and weddings and forever after, he'd just fucked up any chance of them exploring if that love from their teens could grow into something that could last forever.

Zane Calhoun was Cupid's biggest idiot when it came to love and relationships. Skye had sacrificed their love for his dream and he'd gone off to college, blaming her for his heartache.

Chapter Eight

"Hey Skye, where did you and Zane disappear to last night?" Jennifer, one of the bridesmaids asked.

Skye smiled. "If I told you, I'd have to kill you."

Inside her heart was breaking, but she was determined to make certain that her part of Michelle's wedding was perfect. Still, every so often, she'd stop and wipe the moisture from her eyes.

Skye had not returned to Cupid to fall for Zane all over again, but seeing him and tumbling into bed with him, had reopened the wound that had taken so long to heal. And the worst part was that he thought she'd gone to Dallas and never mourned the loss of them.

Well, he could kiss the southern side of a northbound donkey heading for Amarillo for all she cared. As soon as she could pick up Putz, she was out of this one-red-light town and heading back to where she fit in. Where no one commented on her wild hairdo and appreciated her artistic talents.

She sprayed hair spray to hold the style she'd created for Michelle. Skye held up a mirror for Michelle to see the way her hair cascaded over the top of the veils crown.

"What do you think?" she asked, knowing her friend had never looked more beautiful.

"Huh?" Michelle asked, looking up with a dazed expression on her face.

"Are you okay? I mean, I'm sure you've got pre-wedding jitters and all that, but are you feeling all right?"

"I don't know," Michelle cried. "I just don't know."

Skye patted her friend on the arm. "What's wrong, Michelle?"

She blinked her eyes rapidly. "I'm sorry, you've done a

great job. It's perfect, just like I planned. The whole wedding is perfect, just like I planned. It's just pre-wedding jitters."

A knock sounded on the door.

"Who is it," one of the bridesmaids asked, while Michelle retreated back into herself.

"It's Zane. Is Skye in there?"

Skye shook her head vehemently. What the hell did he want now? She didn't want to talk to him. There was nothing left to say.

"She's not here," a bridesmaid lied for her.

"Do you know where she's at?"

Again Skye shook her head.

"No," they called.

They heard him walk away and Skye sighed a huge breath of relief.

Michelle came out of her stupor to stare at her. "Why didn't you talk to him?"

She shrugged. "This is your big day. He can wait."

Michelle frowned at her. "I thought after last night things were good between the two of you."

Skye smiled. "You're getting married in an hour. Any last requests before I start packing up the goods?"

"What happened?"

"Nothing," Skye said, blinking to keep the tears at bay. "We're supposed to be happy. You're about to marry the man of your dreams."

Michelle frowned. "Yes."

A pounding came on the door again. "Skye, I know you're in there. Your car is out front. I've searched the entire church. You have to be in there."

Silence filled the room as everyone looked at her for direction.

"If you don't come out, I'm coming in," Zane said.

Skye didn't say anything. The girls giggled. Everyone

was sitting around in robes, waiting until the last moment before they put their dresses on.

"I mean it. I'm coming in there," he yelled.

Skye rolled her eyes. She stepped away from Michelle, crossed her arms and waited for Zane to make an ass of himself.

It didn't take long.

The door was locked, so he kicked it, causing the lock to break and the door to swing open.

Skye stared at him as he almost fell into the room. "That's quite an entrance you just made."

"You could have opened the door."

"Why? We said everything this morning."

"No, you said everything this morning."

"After you let me know that last night I was just a fuck. That you hoped I hurt the way you hurt when I left. I think we said it all this morning."

The room reeked of silence. The air so thick with tension Skye could hear the other girls in the room breathing. Now everyone knew he'd used her.

She turned away, fighting the tears and the embarrassment of everyone witnessing her humiliation on Valentine's Day.

"Skye," he said, his voice choking up. "Please look at me."

"I can't," she said wishing the darn tears would stop flowing.

"I'm the biggest damn fool in Cupid, Texas. I was young and stupid and I never considered before this morning that you sacrificed our relationship to help me achieve my dream. You knew how much I wanted to become a vet."

He walked up behind her and placed his hand on her arm. At his touch her heart nearly exploded. He was so near and yet so far. Slowly, he turned her to face him. With his thumb, he brushed a tear that ran down her cheek. "I'm sorry for what I said this morning. It wasn't until you left that I realized you were right. We wouldn't have made it if I hadn't gone away to college. I love what I do and I would have been miserable doing manual labor. Though, I would have done it at the time if it meant you stayed beside me."

"I wanted you to be happy. But I thought you'd forgive me and come back to me," Skye said, hope beginning to fill her. "But you never returned for me."

Zane hung his head for a moment and then raised it to meet her gaze head on. "I'm not too bright when it comes to relationships of the heart. Otherwise I wouldn't be standing here apologizing on Valentine's Day. I don't know if we're meant to be together. I'd just like for you to give me a third chance for us to explore this thing between us. Even if it means me moving to Dallas."

Skye felt her heart soar. She couldn't stop the smile from spreading across her face. "Does this mean you don't hate me?"

"Yes," he grimaced. "I never truly hated you. I missed you so much I didn't know how to live without you."

"I waited for you for so long.'

"I wasn't smart enough to realize you would wait. I want another chance for us."

She smiled and stepped into his embrace. She threw her arms around his neck. His mouth covered hers in a kiss that expressed his feelings the way words couldn't.

The room erupted in ahs from the bridesmaids.

<u>Thank you for reading!</u>

Dear Reader,

Thank you so much for reading *Cupid's Revenge.*

Whether you loved the book or hated it, I would appreciate it if you let everyone know by leaving a few words on your favorite vendor's website.

If you enjoy western historical authors, please join the Pioneer Hearts group on Facebook. This is a fabulous group of readers and authors who enjoy westerns.

Sign up for my newsletter at sylviamcdaniel.com if you'd like to learn about my new releases as soon as possible.

Reading one of my books is like spending time with me, and I just want to say thank you from the bottom of my heart.

Yours in Drama, Divas, Bad Boys, and Romance!
Sincerely,
Sylvia McDaniel

Books by Sylvia McDaniel

Contemporary Romance

Standalones
The Reluctant Santa
My Sister's Boyfriend
The Wanted Bride
The Relationship Coach
Her Christmas Lie
Secrets, Lies, and Online Dating
Paying for the Past
Cupid's Revenge

Anthologies
Kisses, Laughter & Love
Christmas with you

Collaborative Series

Magic, New Mexico
Touch of Decadence

Western Historicals

Standalones
A Hero's Heart
A Scarlet Bride
Second Chance Cowboy

The Cuvier Women
Wronged
Betrayed
Beguiled

Lipstick and Lead
Desperate
Deadly
Dangerous
Daring
Determined
Deceived

Scandalous Suffragettes
Abigail
Bella
Callie
Faith

The Burnett Brides
The Rancher Takes a Bride
The Outlaw Takes a Bride
The Marshal Takes a Bride
The Christmas Bride

Anthologies
Wild Western Women
Courting the West
Wild Western Women Ride Again

Collaborative Series

The Surprise Brides
Ethan

American Mail Order Brides
Katie

About the Author

Sylvia McDaniel is a best-selling, award-winning author of historical romance and contemporary romance novels. Known for her sweet, funny, family-oriented romances, Sylvia is the author of The Burnett Brides, a western historical western series, The Cuvier Widows, a Louisiana historical series, and several short contemporary romances.

She is the former President of the Dallas Area Romance Authors, a member of the Romance Writers of America®, and a member of Novelists Inc. Her novel, A Hero's Heart, was a 1996 Golden Heart Finalist. Several other books have placed or won in the San Antonio Romance Authors Contest and the LERA Contest, and she was a Golden Network Finalist.

Married for nearly twenty years to her best friend, they have two dachshunds that are beyond spoiled and a good-looking, grown son who thinks there's no place like home. She loves gardening, shopping, knitting, and football (Cowboys and Bronco's fan), but not necessarily in that order.

Look for her the first Tuesday of every month at the Plotting Princesses blogspot, and be sure to sign up for her newsletter to learn about new releases and contests. Every month a new subscriber is entered into a drawing for a free book!

She can be found online at: www.sylviamcdaniel.com or on Facebook. You can write to Sylvia at P.O. Box 2542, Coppell, TX 7501

Looking for a new book to read?

Nicole Cuvier went to New Orleans to share wonderful news with her husband only to discover him in a hotel room murdered, with two other women claiming to be his wives. It seems there are three Cuvier Widows and each one is suspected of murder.

Pregnant, unmarried, and now a widow with a plantation on the verge of bankruptcy. Nicole needs a temporary husband. Someone to save Rosewood and give her child a last name. Enter a handsome drifter, Maxim Viel, who agrees to marry her, but unbeknownst to Nicole, wants more than a temporary arrangement. Can his strong arms, tender caresses and heated kisses heal her shattered heart? Or could the price of his love, be more than Nicole is willing to give?

Sneak Peek into Betrayed

They Met Over His Dead Body

New Orleans, 1895

For the first time in their marriage, Nicole Rosseau Cuvier disobeyed her husband Jean. Though he told her never to come to his office in New Orleans without him, the news she had simply could not wait. And his office was just several hours by boat down the Mississippi River.

Yet her joy dimmed when she arrived at her husband's shipping company, and the clerk mysteriously informed her that Jean was ill and gave her his room number at the Chateau Hotel.

In the entire four years they'd been married, Jean Cuvier had never been ill.

Nicole burst into the hotel room, uncertain what she would find. Her gaze swept across the open room to a man dressed in a shabby suit in conversation with a refined lady with dark hair and smoky-gray eyes. "Where is he? Is he all right? They told me he was ill."

The man stepped between Nicole and an open door where she could see uniformed men standing around an unidentifiable body stretched out on the floor. Who could that be lying on the floor?

"Who are you?" the man asked, blocking her path.

"I'm Mrs. Cuvier," Nicole said anxiously. "I went by my husband's office and they sent me over here. Is the doctor with him?" she asked, trying to peer around the man to see into the other room.

"Good Lord, another one?" the man muttered, gazing back at the lady he'd been speaking with.

"Who did you say you were?" the woman inquired as she stared at Nicole, her gray eyes large and questioning.

Nicole didn't have time to chitchat with this woman, whoever she was. If Jean were ill, he needed her. "I'm Mrs. Nicole Cuvier, Jean's wife. Now where is my husband?"

The man in the shabby suit coat glanced at the other woman and then turned his gaze on Nicole. "Jean Cuvier is dead."

Nicole felt as if someone punched her in the stomach. With a trembling hand she clutched her throat, trying to hold back the scream that seemed to swell and lodge itself in her throat. The room swayed precariously as a dizzy spell overcame her, the words reverberating through her mind. Her beloved husband was dead.

"No. No," Nicole cried, tears rushing to her eyes, hysteria bubbling up, threatening to overwhelm her. "Dear God, no. He can't be! Let me see him. Please tell me this is a mistake. Where is he?"

"I'll take you to him," the man said, taking Nicole's arm and gently guiding her. "I'm Detective Dunegan, with the New Orleans police."

Nicole heard the words, but her mind didn't comprehend what he was saying. Police detective? What was a detective doing here with her husband? He led her into the bedroom where the same body she'd seen earlier lay sprawled on the floor, surrounded by people.

Please, God, that couldn't be Jean.

She caught a glimpse of dark hair tinted with silver, the color of Jean's hair. The man wore pajamas the same dark brown that Jean loved, a silk robe wrapped around his still form.

At the detective's motion, they moved aside and let her in close to see the man she loved, who lay twisted on the floor, his skin an odd pinkish hue that looked unnatural. She knelt beside him, her hand reaching out as her fingers touched his cold flesh. Quickly, she drew her hand back, the sensation confirming that her husband's lifeblood no longer flowed, his warm, loving touch now just a memory. A sob tore from her throat as she gazed at Jean, feeling as if this couldn't be real.

Gently the detective helped her up from the floor and led her back into the main room of the hotel suite. Nicole sobbed for her husband, who'd taught her so much about life. Their short time together had been filled with love and laughter, and even today she'd come bringing him such joyous news.

"I think we need to remain calm, sit down, and find out what happened," the officer said, his voice firm and reassuring.

Calm? How could she remain calm when she'd just found out her husband was dead? That no longer would he hold her in his arms or his smiles brighten her day.

"What—what. . . happened?" Nicole sobbed, tears streaking down her face. "How did he die?"

"Poisoning. We suspect that his wi—the woman we found him with poisoned him."

Nicole spun around and glared at the finely dressed woman through tear-streaked eyes. Could she be Jean's killer?

Her large gray eyes returned her gaze unflinchingly. "Not me. There's another woman."

"What do you mean, another woman?" Nicole asked, confused.

"You're not the only Mrs. Cuvier in this hotel suite," the woman advised her.

Another Mrs. Cuvier? What was she talking about? Nicole didn't understand. The only other Mrs. Cuvier was a distant relative of Jean's who lived hundreds of miles away. Why were they lying to her?

"I don't believe you," Nicole said, fear making her almost hysterical.

The detective took Nicole by the arm and motioned for the other woman to follow him. They walked into an adjoining room where a young woman sat staring off at the horizon, her dark eyes glazed and distant.

"Layla," the detective said, releasing Nicole. "Tell these women how the man you're suspected of killing was related to you."

She turned her oval-shaped face toward the door. Hair black as night was swept up off her neck in a coiffure that left wisps of curls swirling around her pale face. She turned dark, censorious eyes on the detective and raised her brows in a disdainful look that was both elegant and disapproving. "I told you I did not kill my husband."

Nicole moaned, the woman's words confirming her worst fears, yet she couldn't believe this was happening. There had to be a mistake. "What are you saying? No! You lie. You can't be married to Jean."

The girl glanced briefly at Nicole, not responding.

"Did you marry Jean Cuvier?" the distinguished woman asked her.

"Yes," the young girl said, her voice starting to tremble. Her bright red lips pouted.

"That can't be. He married me. He's my husband," Nicole said, her voice rising, the pain and hurt audible in her voice, unable to control the fear that raged through her.

"And mine," the woman said quietly as she sank down onto a nearby chair. "I'm Marian Cuvier. I married him twelve years ago at Saint Ann's Cathedral."

Nicole turned abruptly and stared at her in disbelief. "No. That's impossible." She paused, comprehension as fleeting as the wind. "No. We were married four years ago. I don't understand. He would never do something so horrible."

"And I married him a year ago," Layla whispered, her face turning ashen.

"Impossible. Jean loved me. That's . . . that's bigamy!" Nicole said, shaking her head from side to side. Jean would never hurt her this way. He loved her. He told her over and over how he loved her more than any other woman.

"Yes, it is bigamy. We're all married to the same man," Marian replied, her voice sounding uncaring and cold. "And now we're all Jean's widows. The Cuvier Widows."

Nicole sobbed. Dear God, she'd come to town to tell Jean that after four years she finally was expecting their baby. And instead she'd learned that the father of her child, the man she loved with all her heart, was a bigamist—and he'd been murdered.